Enid B

A FARAWAY TREE
Adventure

In SANTA CLAUS'S
CASTLE

A. P.
Olivia, George and Fred

EGMONT

We bring stories to life

Cover and interior illustrations by Alex Paterson

Text first published in Great Britain by Newnes as chapter 4
of The Enid Blyton Omnibus! 1952
Published as In Santa Claus's Castle: A Faraway Tree Adventure 2016
by Egmont UK Limited
2 Minster Court, 10th floor, London EC3R 7BB
Text copyright © 1952 Hodder & Stoughton Ltd.
ENID BLYTON ® Copyright © 2016 Hodder & Stoughton Ltd.
ENID BLYTON ® Illustrations Copyright © 2016 Hodder & Stoughton Ltd.

ISBN 978 1 4052 80112

www.egmont.co.uk

A CIP catalogue record for this title is available from the British Library

Printed in Singapore

62861/007

Stay safe online. Any website addresses listed in this book are correct
at the time of going to print. However, Egmont is not responsible
for content hosted by third parties. Please be aware that online content
can be subject to change and websites can contain content
that is unsuitable for children. We advise that all children are
supervised when using the internet.

Egmont takes its responsibility to the planet and its inhabitants very seriously.
We aim to use papers from well-managed forests run by responsible suppliers.

Enid Blyton

A FARAWAY TREE
Adventure

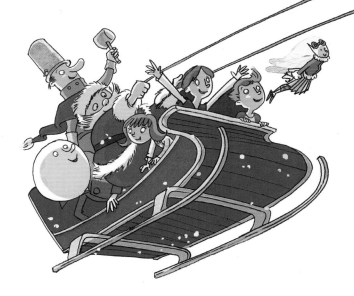

In SANTA CLAUS'S
CASTLE

EGMONT

The World of the
FARAWAY TREE

MOON-FACE lives at the very top. In his house is the start of the **SLIPPERY-SLIP**, a huge slide that curves all the way down inside the trunk of the tree.

SILKY lives below Moon-Face. She is the prettiest little fairy you ever did see.

SAUCEPAN MAN is a funny old thing. His saucepans make lots of noise when they jangle together, so he can't hear very well.

CHAPTER ONE
The Saucepan Man Brings News

KNOCKITY-KNOCK-KNOCK!

'Good gracious! It sounds as if somebody's at the door!' said Joe. 'I'll go and open it, Mother.'

He went to open the door – there stood the Old Saucepan Man. He was hung about with pots and pans and kettles as usual, and had a saucepan for a hat.

'Hello,' said the Saucepan Man, 'didn't you hear me knock? I've come to tell you that we must go **to the top of the Faraway Tree** tomorrow. There's a very nice land coming there.'

'What is it?' asked Joe.

'Toyland,' said Saucepan. 'You could bring a bag with you and collect quite a lot in time for Christmas.'

'Oh what a good idea!' said Joe. He called to his two sisters. 'Beth! Frannie! Did you hear what the Saucepan Man said?'

'Yes!' they cried running to the door. 'Oh, Saucepan, we really must come. Can we help ourselves to toys, do you think?'

'Well, I've an aunt there,' said Saucepan, 'and if I tell her you're my friends, you can have what you want. Can you meet me at the top of the Faraway Tree tomorrow morning?'

'Oh, yes – and will **Moon-Face and Silky** be coming too?' asked Beth, happily. 'We haven't seen them for ages.'

'We'll have fun!' said Frannie.

'Yes, please,' said Saucepan unexpectedly. 'I'd like one very much.'

'Like what?' said Beth, astonished.

'What you just offered me – a bun,' said Saucepan, looking round for it.

'Oh – you suddenly went deaf,' said Beth. 'I just said – **we'll have FUN.**'

'Oh! All the same **I'd like a bun,**' said
Saucepan.

Joe got him a bun out of the cake-tin.

He went off, munching happily, his pans
rattling and **clanging** round him. 'See
you tomorrow!' he called.

The next day the three children came to the Faraway Tree in the middle of the wood. It looked even more enormous than usual. It towered up **into the clouds,** and the children couldn't even see the top of it. Its trunk was so big that it was quite a walk to go all the way round it!

'Great! The tree's growing blackberries today,' said Joe, picking some big ripe ones.

'Well, it shouldn't then,' said Beth.

'Blackberries grow on bushes, not on trees. The Faraway Tree's made a mistake!'

They began to climb the tree. A little way up it stopped growing **blackberries** and grew **pine-cones!**

'Not so good,' said Joe. 'We can't eat pine-cones, Faraway Tree.'

'It's a very exciting tree, this,' said Frannie. 'Always growing different things all the way up – and having people living in it too – and a slippery-slip all the way inside from the top to the bottom. I'm glad we live near a tree like this. **We're lucky.**'

'Yes. I bet a lot of children wish they lived near it too,' said Joe, helping Beth over a steep bit.

They climbed right up to
Moon-Face's little door. Moon-
Face opened it, beaming all over
his big round face. **'Oh, come in,'**
he said.

'We're just having a snack
before we go. **Well-I-Never
Rolls.'**

'**What a peculiar name,**' said Joe, looking at the dish of nice crusty little rolls. '**What do they taste of?**'

'Try one,' said Moon-Face. 'And tell us!'

Joe took a roll and bit into it. 'Tastes of cheese,' he said. 'No — well I never, it tastes of ginger now. No, it doesn't — it's chocolate! And now it tastes of coconut — **well I never!**'

'**Yes. Most peculiar, isn't it?**' said
Moon-Face. 'No wonder they're called
Well-I-Never Rolls. Every chew you have
tastes of something different.'

'Jolly good,' said Joe. 'I'll have another.
My – this tastes of **pickled onions** – no,
it doesn't – **it's custard** – lovely!'

Saucepan bit into his. 'Ah – mint! Delicious! Why, it's mint sauce, I can taste the tiny bits of mint.'

'You'll find you've got roast lamb next,' said Silky.

Saucepan looked surprised. 'No – it isn't ham,' he said.

'I said LAMB!' shouted Silky.

'No, it's not jam,' said Saucepan. 'Well I never, it's lamb! Lamb and mint sauce – how clever! **Really these rolls are remarkable.'**

So they were. The six of them finished up the whole dish of them. 'I wish I'd brought heaps more,' said Saucepan, getting up. **'Well, aren't we going up to Toyland?** Do hurry up.'

13

CHAPTER TWO
The Land of Toys

They were all ready. They went out
of Moon-Face's little round room and
climbed up the **topmost branch** into a
cloud. They came to the little ladder that
led upwards through the last bit of cloud.
Toyland should be at the top!

Saucepan went first. He climbed off the top rung of the ladder, and called down to the others. **'Yes, it's here. Come on!'**

Up they all went, and at last stood in Toyland. But there seemed to be no toys about at all. Saucepan pointed to a town not far off. Flags were flying brightly from little houses.

'There's the **Village of Toys**,' he said. 'Now we'll go and find my aunt.'

They set off to the village. But when they got there, Saucepan stopped and looked **puzzled.**

'Dear me,' he said, 'this isn't the land I hoped. **The toys are all alive** – look, isn't that a teddy bear walking about?'

'Yes,' said Beth. **'Goodness** – we can't take toys like these away to play with at home! They're as big as we are!'

'I'll find my aunt,' said Saucepan, and they all walked down the village street, meeting three or four sailor dolls, a curious man who had no legs but just wobbled along, and some beautifully dressed dolls.

Saucepan's aunt was nowhere to be found.

'Your aunt lives in the other land, you silly,' said Silky. 'This must be the **Land of Toys,** not Toyland.'

20

'Oh, well — let's enjoy ourselves, anyway,' said Saucepan. 'Here comes another wobbly man. Let's try and push him over.'

The wobbly man was astonished and annoyed when Saucepan gave him a push. He wobbled over backwards and then came forwards again, only to get another push, this time from Moon-Face.

'How dare you?' cried the wobbly man in a rage. 'That's not the way for visitors to behave! I'll report you to the Captain of the Toy Soldiers!'

He wobbled off at a remarkable speed. The three children and Silky felt a bit scared.

'You shouldn't go round pushing people, Saucepan,' said Joe. 'Not even to see them wobble. I do hope we don't get into trouble.'

'Look — there's the Captain of the Soldiers,' said Beth, afraid.

'And the Wobbly Man is with him. He's complained about us, as he said he would. **We'd better run away.'**

22

'No,' said Joe. 'We can easily explain, and Saucepan must say he's sorry.'

Up marched the toy soldier, **as smart as could be.**

'You must come with me,' said the Captain, in a commanding voice. 'You are not toys, and should not be here. Also, your behaviour must be looked into. Follow me, quick **MARCH!'**

'We'd better follow,' said Joe. 'He can't do anything to us; he's only a toy, even if he is alive. And I must say I'd rather like to see what that toy fort is like inside.'

The Captain took them through the village and up to the wooden fort. It was very like a toy fort that Joe had once had. It even had a **wooden drawbridge** that could be pulled up or let down.

It was let down for them to walk over. Toy cannons stood here and there. Joe went up to one. **'Funny old cannon!'** he said. 'Look, there's a knob to pull back and then let go, just like the toy cannon I had in my little fort at home.'

He pulled back the knob, let it go and then **BANG!** The cannon went off with a loud noise!

The wobbly man was so shocked that
he almost fell over, and it took a lot of
wobbles for him to stand upright again.

The toys in the village below were so
frightened when the cannon went **BANG**
that they rushed out of their little houses
and ran for their lives! The Captain was
very angry indeed.

'Now see what you've done!' he said
to Joe. 'Let off the cannon, and scared
everybody! You must be mad.'

'I'm very sorry,' said Joe. 'I never thought
the cannon would go off like that.'

'Well, what did you think it would do?'
said the Captain, angrily. **'Whistle a
tune or dance a jig?'**

Nobody dared to laugh.

The Captain led them on again.

Soon they came to a door that led into
a **wooden tower.** They went in and
found themselves in a room with a table
and a chair at one end, and nothing else.
The Captain sat himself down in the
chair. 'Stand up straight,' he said. Everyone
stood up very straight, even Saucepan.

'**Salute,**' said the Captain, and
everyone saluted, though Moon-Face used
the wrong hand.

'**Dismiss!**' said the Captain, and everyone stared. What did he mean?

'No – that's wrong,' said the Captain. 'Don't dismiss. **Stand at ease.**'

They obeyed. The Captain rapped loudly on the table. 'You are accused of not being toys. You are accused of punching wobbly men. You are accused of setting off cannons. You –'

'Only one wobbly man, and one cannon,' said Joe. **'We're sorry and we won't do it again.** We'll dismiss now!'

But before they could go they heard the noise of marching feet, and into the room came about fifty toy soldiers, all very wooden. They surrounded the children and the others.

'To the **deepest dungeon** with them!' shouted the Captain.

'NO!' shouted Joe, and he pushed the nearest soldier hard. The soldier fell against the soldier next to him and knocked him over. That one fell against the next one and he went down, too, knocking the soldier next to him – and before five seconds had passed every soldier was lying flat on the floor.

'It's like **playing dominoes** – knock the first over, and down goes the whole row!' said Frannie with a **giggle.**

The Captain looked alarmed. What was he to do with people like these? Goodness – one push, and all his soldiers were down!

'Now listen,' said the Captain. 'Either you become toys, or you go to the **deepest dungeon.** You can choose.'

'All right – we'll be toys, then!' said Joe with a grin. **'I'll be a clockwork clown, and go head-over-heels all the time!'**

'Right – you're a clockwork clown,' said the Captain. 'What will you be?' and he pointed at Moon-Face.

'**A teddy bear,**' grinned Moon-Face, 'with a **growl** in my middle.' And he pressed himself in the middle and pretended to **growl**.

'I'll be a doll,' said Silky, and began to walk about stiffly like a doll.

'**And I'll be a furry grey rabbit!**' said the Saucepan Man. 'I'll grow long floppy ears and grey fur!'

'We'll be dolls,' said Beth and Frannie together, and they walked about stiffly like Silky, giggling all the time.

'Right,' said the Captain thankfully. 'You are now toys, and can remain in the Land of Toys. **Dis-MISS!**'

The six of them went out laughing, Joe still turning **head-over-heels,** just for fun.

CHAPTER THREE
Real Toys

Frannie was just going to say something to Saucepan, who was in front of her, when she stopped. She stared hard.

She saw **something very peculiar.** Saucepan wore a saucepan for a hat, as usual – but, goodness, he had suddenly grown two huge floppy ears! The saucepan sat on top, looking very odd.

'Saucepan,' said Frannie, astonished. 'Saucepan, what's wrong with you?'

Saucepan turned round, surprised, and everyone got a tremendous shock. His face was covered in grey fur and **he had very long whiskers!**

'He's a toy rabbit!' said Frannie, with a squeal. 'Saucepan – **you're a toy rabbit!** You said you would be, and now you are.'

They were all very surprised. They stared and stared at poor Saucepan.

Saucepan looked at himself in one of his bright pans, which he used as a mirror. He was shocked to see such a furry face looking back at him. He gazed round at the others, scared.

Then he gave a shout and pointed to Joe. 'Well! Look at him! He's a clockwork clown now, hat and all! Yes, and he's got a key in

his back! **Joe, you're a clown!** No wonder you keep going **head-over-heels!'**

Joe turned another somersault at once. The others gazed at him. Yes, Joe was a clown, with a clown's hat and suit. His face was daubed in red and white like a clown's too.

Frannie looked at the others, and **squealed** again. 'Look at Moon-Face – he's a **fat, round little teddy bear,** with a round, teddy-bear face that's hardly like Moon-Face's at all!'

'Oh dear,' said Moon-Face, putting up his hand to feel his face. 'I've gone all furry. Where are my clothes? They've gone.'

Joe pressed him in the middle and an alarming growl came out – **grrrrrrrrr!**

'Don't,' said Silky. 'You made me jump. Don't press him again, Joe. Oh, my goodness – this is dreadful. We're all toys. Look at me!'

You're not so bad,' said Joe, looking at her. 'You are the prettiest doll I ever saw. And Beth and Frannie are dolls, too. Look at them walking about, as stiff as can be.'

'Yes, we're really toys,' said Frannie. 'It must have begun to happen when we said we'd be toys, and chose what we'd be. But we only said it for fun.'

'I know. **But you never know what will happen** in the lands that come to the top of the Faraway Tree,' said Joe. 'Moon-Face, will we stop being toys when we get out of this land?'

'No, I don't think so,' said the teddy bear. 'And anyway, how do you think you are going to **head-over-heels down the Faraway Tree?** We'll just have to hope this will all wear off.'

'I don't like being a toy rabbit,' said Saucepan sadly.

'Oh, come on,' said Joe, going head-over-heels again. 'Let's explore the **Village of Toys** and hope all this wears off. If only I didn't have to go head-over-heels so often! I'm getting very tired of it.'

'So are we,' said Frannie, getting out of his way. 'Do keep over there, Joe – you'll knock me over.'

They came to a little garage. A very
furry rabbit was busy putting petrol into
a car driven by another toy rabbit. They
looked at Saucepan in surprise as he came
along with the others.

'Hello!' said the garage rabbit. 'What's
the idea of wearing a saucepan for a
hat? I can't say I've ever seen **a rabbit
wearing a hat** before.'

'**Well, you've seen one now,**' said Saucepan, not very politely. 'Bother these awful floppy ears. I hate them. They make me look like a toy rabbit.'

'Well, you are a toy rabbit, floppy ears and all,' said the rabbit, staring.

'That's where you're wrong,' said
Saucepan. 'I'm not. I hate being one.
Ugly creatures, with stupid long ears and
quivering whiskers!'

'Stop it, Saucepan,' said Joe, in a
warning voice. He turned to the surprised
rabbit. 'You must excuse him,' he said, 'he's
really a **Saucepan Man,** as you can see.

And I'm not really a clockwork clown,
I'm a boy.'

'I see,' said the rabbit. 'Well, I should just
hate to be an ugly little Saucepan Man, so
I know what he feels about being a rabbit
– though **rabbits are very handsome
creatures** – like myself. He should be
pleased he's turned into one.'

'**Well, we really like being ourselves best,**' said Frannie. 'I'm a little girl, not a doll. And this teddy bear is really Moon-Face.'

'Never heard of him,' said the rabbit. 'Didn't know there were such things as Moon-Faces.'

Frannie **giggled.** Silky went up to the rabbit and smiled at him. 'Please do help us,' she said.

The rabbit stared at her. He thought she was the prettiest doll he had ever seen in the Village of Toys.

The rabbit who was inside the car leaned out. **'Of course we'll help you,'** he said. 'What do you want us to do?'

'Well, we did hope all this would wear off,' said Silky in a high doll's voice. 'But it hasn't. And we wondered if you knew how we could get back into ourselves again.'

The two rabbits looked at one another. 'Difficult,' said one.

'Very,' said the other.

'What about **the old Spell-Maker, Mr Oom-Boom-Boom?**' said the first one. 'If he's in a good mood, he might do something for them.'

'Yes. But if he's in a bad mood, he might turn them into something worse,' said the second rabbit.

'Then we won't go there,' said Joe hurriedly, and **turned a somersault.**

'We could see if he's in a good or bad mood before we say anything,' said the rabbit. 'I'll take you there in my car, if you can all squeeze in.'

'Well, we could try,' said Moon-Face, his little round teddy-bear face looking worried.

The rabbit told Silky to sit next to him. He thought she was really beautiful, and very sweet. 'I am sure, if you went to ask **Mr Oom-Boom-Boom** a favour he would say "yes" at once,' he said. 'I never saw anyone as pretty as you.'

'Well you're a very handsome rabbit,' said Silky, and that pleased him very much. **They all squeezed into the car somehow** and set off.

CHAPTER FOUR
Mr Oom-Boom-Boom

Nobody talked after that except Silky and the toy rabbit. The car went on and on, and at last Joe wanted to get out and go **head-over-heels** again.

'Can you stop?' he called.

'Goodness, I've gone right past Mr Oom-Boom-Boom!' said the rabbit, putting on the brake so suddenly that **the saucepan flew off Saucepan's head** and rolled away down the road. 'Yes, get out and somersault for a bit while I turn the car round.'

So Joe turned about **ten somersaults,**
while the toy rabbit turned the car round.
Then back they went to find Mr Oom-
Boom-Boom.

'Don't start talking to Silky or you'll go right past again,' begged Frannie. But this time the rabbit kept an eye open for Mr Oom-Boom-Boom's house and suddenly put on the brakes again.

They stared at a **funny little door** set in a grassy hill. On it was printed in bold black letters:

OOM-BOOM-BOOM. KNOCK SEVEN TIMES.

'Silky, you go,' said Frannie. 'Perhaps Oom-Boom-Boom will be nice to you. You really do look very sweet.'

'All right. I'll knock,' said Silky bravely, though she felt very scared. She got out of the car, and went up to the little door. She took hold of the knocker and knocked seven times – **blam-blam-blam-blam-blam-blam-blam!**

A loud voice came from inside. 'Stop knocking. Once is quite enough!'

'Oh dear – he's in a bad mood!' called the rabbit. 'Come back quickly, Silky, and we'll drive off.'

'I can't come,' wailed Silky. **'The knocker has got hold of my hand. It won't let go!'**

Joe jumped out at once and went to help her. But Silky was quite right. The knocker had tight hold of her hand and wouldn't let it go.

Moon-Face went to help, too, and then the Saucepan Man, looking very worried. And just at that very moment the door opened, pulling poor Silky with it, and a voice **boomed** out loudly: 'What's all this? Disturbing me in the middle of my spells!'

Everyone thought that Oom-Boom-Boom was a very good name for him, **booming** at them like that.

But he wasn't a bit like his voice. He was an old pixie **with a beard so long that it trailed behind him.** He had big, pointed ears, and wore **a funny little round hat** with feelers on it like a butterfly's. His eyes were as green as grass and very bright indeed.

He frowned at them all – and then he saw Silky, still held by the knocker.

'Ah,' he said, and a smile broke over his face **like the sun shining out suddenly.** 'Ah! What a dear little doll! No wonder my knocker wouldn't let you go. I've never seen a doll as pretty as you! Do you know where you ought to be?'

'No,' said Silky, with a gasp.

'You ought to be standing at the very top of the **great big Christmas Tree that Santa Claus** has in his castle!' said Oom-Boom-Boom. 'He's always looking for the prettiest doll in the world to put there, but he's never found one as pretty as you yet!'

'I'm not a doll,' said Silky. **'I'm a fairy.** I've been turned into a doll today.'

'Let her go, knocker,' said the pixie. 'Come in, all of you. Why have you paid me this visit?'

'He seems in a **very good mood** now,' whispered Joe to Moon-Face. 'I think it's safe to go in.'

CHAPTER FIVE
Poor Silky

Inside there was a **narrow, very winding** passage that led into the hill. They followed the pixie down it, everybody

stumbling over his **very long beard** that
trailed out behind him.

He took them to a big room with a
very low ceiling. A great fire burned in the
middle, but the flames were green, not red,
and no heat came from them.

'I was just making a few spells,' said Oom-Boom-Boom, his big voice **echoing** all round the room. **'I'm a spell-maker, you know.'**

'Yes. That's why we came,' said Silky, feeling very nervous. 'Please, dear Mr Oom-Boom-Boom, will you use a spell to help us? We want to go back to our right selves. I'm a fairy, really, as I told you.'

'And we're really little girls,' said Beth and Frannie. 'And this clown is a boy, and the toy rabbit is Old Saucepan Man . . .'

'And I'm Moon-Face,' said Moon-Face, his little teddy-bear face looking very earnest. **'Please do help us.'**

'Ha,' said Oom-Boom-Boom, looking round at them and **beaming**, 'well, I don't mind doing that. That's easy. But **I'll do it on one condition.'**

'What's that?' asked Joe, his heart sinking.

'I'll turn five of you back to your own shapes — but I want this little doll here to stay with me so that I can sell her to **Santa Claus** to put on the top of his Christmas Tree! It will be such an honour for her. You'd love that, wouldn't you, my dear?' he said to Silky, turning to her.

Silky looked very frightened. 'Well — I'll stay and let you sell me to Santa Claus,' she said, 'if you will use a spell on the others.'

'Oh, dear, darling Silky!' said Moon-Face, putting his furry arm round her, 'How sweet you are! But we wouldn't let you. **We'd never leave you here alone.'**

'Never, never, never, never,' said Joe, Beth and Frannie.

'I'm going to stay,' said Silky, looking as if she was going to cry, but smiling at them all the same. 'It won't be so bad, going to Santa Claus, though it sounds very dull standing on the top of his Christmas Tree. **But it's for you, so I want to do it!'**

'Of course she wants to do it,' said Oom-Boom-Boom. 'She's a sensible little doll.'

'Be quiet,' said Joe. 'I tell you we won't let her do it! We'd rather be toys all our lives than that!'

Then Mr Oom-Boom-Boom lost his temper. He rushed at Joe – but Joe did a very clever thing. He caught him by his very long beard, dragged him to a big table and tied him to it with his beard, **making dozens of knots!**

'Now, quick, let's go!' he cried. 'Sorry about tying you up, Oom-Boom-Boom, but you're not going to have Silky. **Run everyone!'**

They ran up the winding passage and came out on the hillside. And oh, thank goodness, there was the rabbit waiting in his car!

Joe got to the car first. **'Quick!'** he cried. 'I can hear Oom-Boom-Boom coming! He must have got free.'

So he had! He appeared at the door of his peculiar house, and they saw that he had freed himself by cutting his beard short. **He did look strange.**

The toy rabbit revved up his car and it shot off.

After they had gone a good way the rabbit stopped the car for a talk, and Joe took the chance of turning about **a dozen somersaults.**

'You know, I think you should go to the **Land of Santa Claus,'** said the rabbit. 'Not to give him Silky, of course, that would never do – but to tell him you aren't toys

and to ask him if he can stop you

being what you're not.'

'**That's a bit muddling,**' said Moon-Face, trying to work it out. 'Yes — it seems a good idea. After all, he deals in toys, doesn't he? He must know them very well. He'll be able to tell we're not real toys, and might help us.'

'**We know he's kind,**' said Silky. 'He's so fond of children. Let's go to him. How can we get there, though?

'I can drive you to the next station and put you on a train for the Land of Santa Claus,' said the toy rabbit. 'I happened to notice that some trains there do go to his land. What about it, friends?'

'**A very good idea,**' said everyone, and off they went. They came to a funny little station after a while, and they all got out.

'I wish you could stay in my land for ever, Silky doll,' said the rabbit to Silky. 'You really are the prettiest thing I ever saw. But you'd be unhappy and I couldn't bear that.'

'I'll write to you,' said Silky.

'Will you really?' said the rabbit. 'Do you know, I've never had a letter in my life! It would make me feel important! Look, there's a train in!'

'Wow! This train's going to the Land of Santa Claus! **What a bit of luck!**' cried Moon-Face. 'Goodbye, rabbit. You really have been a good friend.'

'Goodbye,' said Joe, shaking his furry hand warmly. 'It's been lovely meeting you.'

Silky gave him a kiss and he nearly cried for joy. 'I've never been kissed before,' he said. 'Never. A kiss – and letters – my goodness, **I am a lucky rabbit!**'

They all climbed into the train and waved goodbye.

'Nice fellow, that rabbit,' said Joe. 'Well, we're off again. I wonder how far it is.'

CHAPTER SIX
The Land of Santa Claus

It was quite a long way, and they all fell asleep. A porter woke them up at last.

'Hey, you! Don't you want to get out here?' he said. 'This is where toys usually get out.'

They scrambled out because the station board said, 'Get out here for **the Castle of Santa Claus!**'

'Just in time,' said Joe, yawning. 'Oh – here I go, turning head-over-heels again!'

'There's the castle – look!' said Beth, pointing to **a magnificent castle with many towers,** rising high on a hill nearby. 'And, goodness – **look at the snow!** Anyone would think it was winter here.'

'Oh, it always is,' said the porter. 'It wouldn't be much good for sleighs, would it, if there wasn't snow? Is Santa Claus expecting you? His sleigh usually meets the train in case there are any visitors for him.'

'Is that it down there?' asked Moon-Face, pointing down into the snowy station yard.

A sleigh was there, with four lovely reindeer, whose bells **jingled** as they moved restlessly. A small red pixie held the reins.

'Yes, that's the sleigh. Better go and get in,' said the porter.

They went to the sleigh and got into it. **'To Santa Claus, please,'** said Joe, and off they went, gliding smoothly over the snow, drawn by the four eager reindeer.

They arrived at the castle. They felt rather nervous when they saw how big and grand it was. They stood at an enormous door, carved with all kinds of toys, and **rang** a great bell.

The door swung open. 'Please come in,' said a teddy bear, dressed like a footman. **'Santa Claus will see you in a few minutes.'**

They went into a big hall and then into a great room, **where many little pixies and goblins were at work.**

'You might like to look round while you're waiting,' said the bear footman. 'You'll see the pixies painting the dolls' houses, and the goblins putting **growls** into us bears, and you'll see how the somersaults are put into the clockwork clowns.'

They stood at a safe distance, watching. It was very interesting indeed. So many things were going on; **there was so much to see and hear,** that they almost forgot they were toys themselves.

'How's your **growl**, bear?' said a little pixie, running up to Moon-Face.

He pressed him in the middle and Moon-Face growled deeply. **'Grrrrrr!** Leave me alone! I don't like people doing that.'

'Look – oh, look – **isn't that Santa Claus himself?'** cried Beth, suddenly, as a big man came into the room dressed in bright red. He wore a hood trimmed with white, and his jolly face had eyes that twinkled brightly.

'Yes. It's Santa Claus!' cried Joe. Santa Claus heard him and came over at once. He looked in surprise at Silky.

'Why!' he said, 'where did you come from? You weren't made in my castle, by **pixies and goblins.** You are the loveliest doll I've ever seen. I've a good mind to keep you for myself and put you at the very top of my own big Christmas Tree.'

'No, no, please not!' said Silky.

Santa Claus looked down at the others.
He seemed puzzled.

'Where do you all come from?' he said.
'I am quite sure I have never had any toys
made like you. The rabbit, dressed up in
kettles and saucepans, for instance – and
this **funny little bear.** He doesn't seem
like a proper teddy.'

'We're not proper toys!' said Beth. 'Santa Claus, we got turned into toys in the fort of the toy soldiers. I'm a little girl really.'

'And I'm Moon-Face, who lives at **the top of the Faraway Tree,**' said Moon-Face.

'What! The famous Moon-Face, who has a slippery-slip in his room, going down the tree from the top to the bottom!' cried Santa Claus. 'My goodness – **I've often wanted to see that!** Do you think I'm too fat to go down it?'

'No – no, I don't think so,' said Moon-Face, looking at him. 'I could give you two cushions to sit on instead of one. If you'd like to come now, you can go up and down the Faraway Tree as often

as you like – we'll haul you up in the washing basket every time you arrive at the bottom!'

'Let's go now,' said Santa Claus in delight. 'Well, well – to think I'm meeting the famous Moon-Face at last! And I suppose this lovely doll is Silky the fairy. And, of course – this is the Old Saucepan Man!'

'But – how do you know us?' asked Moon-Face, astonished.

'Oh, I've heard about you from the children,' said Santa Claus. 'They keep asking me for books about you, to go into their Christmas stockings, and they looked **so exciting** that I read them all!'

Well, wasn't that a bit of luck? Santa
Claus called his sleigh and they all got
in. **'To the top of the Faraway Tree,'**
commanded Santa Claus,
and away they went.

CHAPTER SEVEN
Santa and the Slippery-Slip

It didn't take very long. In quite a little while the sleigh landed on a broad bough near the top of the tree, and they all got out.

'My room is just a bit higher up,' said Moon-Face, and led the way. They were soon in his little round room. He pointed to the curious hole in the middle of the floor.

'There you are,' he said. **'That's the slippery-slip** – you fly out of the trapdoor at the bottom, and land on a soft cushion of moss.'

'Splendid!' said Santa Claus. 'Will somebody else go first, please? Goodness, it's exactly the same as I read about in the books!'

'Er – do you think you could just
change us back to our ordinary selves?'
asked Joe, afraid that in his excitement
Santa Claus might forget to do what they
so badly wanted. 'I feel as if I'm going to
somersault again, and I don't want to turn
head-over-heels all the way down the
slippery-slip.'

'Change you back? Yes, of course; it's

easy!' said Santa Claus. **'The slippery-slip is just the right place for a spell.** Shut your eyes, please.'

They all shut their eyes. Santa Claus touched each one gently, chanting a curious little song:

'Go in as you are, Come out as you were, Go in as you are, Come out as you were!'

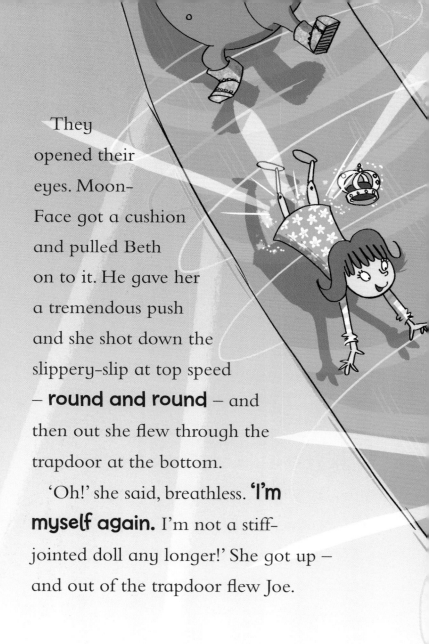

They opened their eyes. Moon-Face got a cushion and pulled Beth on to it. He gave her a tremendous push and she shot down the slippery-slip at top speed – **round and round** – and then out she flew through the trapdoor at the bottom.

'Oh!' she said, breathless. **'I'm myself again.** I'm not a stiff-jointed doll any longer!' She got up – and out of the trapdoor flew Joe.

'Joe! You're all right again! **You're you!'** cried Beth in delight. 'And here comes Silky — she's not a doll any more — and here's Frannie — she's all right, too. Look out — here's the Old Saucepan Man — **yippee,** he's back to normal!'

And then,

Whooooooooooosh!

The trapdoor shot open with a bang
and out sailed Santa Claus!

Bump! He went on to the cushion
of moss, and sat there, panting and full
of delight. **'WHAT a thrill!** Better than
anything I've got in my castle.'

'Look out! Here comes Moon-Face!'
cried Joe, and out came Moon-Face,
no longer a fat teddy bear, but his own
beaming self once more.

'I'd like to do that again,' said Santa
Claus, standing up. 'How did you say
we got back to the top of the tree?
In a basket?'

'Yes,' said Joe, 'but if you don't mind, we won't come with the others. You see, our mother will be wondering about us. So we'd better say goodbye and thank you very much.'

'Goodbye. **See you next Christmas,**' said Santa Claus. 'I'll bring you something extra nice.'

The last thing that Joe, Beth and Frannie saw was Santa Claus in the big basket, being pulled slowly up by all the **squirrels** at the top of the tree.

Moon-Face and Silky and Saucepan were with him, leaning over the edge of the basket, waving to them.

'Well — I suppose dear old Santa Claus will be going down that slippery-slip till it's dark,' said Joe.

'Goodness, wasn't that an adventure!' said Beth.

'We'll never have a better one,' said Frannie.

Oh yes, you will, Frannie, Beth and Joe. **You just wait and see!**

The FARAWAY TREE Adventures

Collect them all!

Each book a classic short story
from the magical Faraway Tree series
with exciting new colour illustrations